OLIVIA™
Plants a Garden

adapted by Emily Sollinger
based on the screenplay written by Rachel Ruderman
and Laurie Israel
illustrated by Jared Osterhold

Ready-to-Read

Simon Spotlight
New York   London   Toronto   Sydney

Based on the TV series *OLIVIA*™ as seen on Nickelodeon™

SIMON SPOTLIGHT
An imprint of Simon & Schuster Children's Publishing Division
1230 Avenue of the Americas, New York, New York 10020
OLIVIA Plants a Garden © 2010 Classic Media, LLC. All rights reserved.
OLIVIA™ Ian Falconer Ink Unlimited, Inc. and © 2010 Ian Falconer and Classic Media, LLC.
All rights reserved.
All rights reserved, including the right of reproduction in whole or in part in any form.
SIMON SPOTLIGHT, READY-TO-READ, and colophon are registered trademarks of Simon & Schuster, Inc.
For information about special discounts for bulk purchases, please contact Simon & Schuster
Special Sales at 1-866-506-1949 or business@simonandschuster.com.
Manufactured in the United States of America 0217 LAK
First Simon Spotlight edition, January 2011
3 4 5 6 7 8 9 10
ISBN 978-1-4424-2011-3 (hc)
ISBN 978-1-4424-1675-8 (pbk)

"It is springtime, children!"
says Mrs. Hoggenmuller.
"We will plant our own gardens.

"Each student will get
a packet of seeds.
You will plant
the seeds at home."

"What will we grow?"
asks Olivia.
"Sprouts, herbs, flowers,
and beans,"
says Mrs. Hoggenmuller.
"Come choose your seeds!"

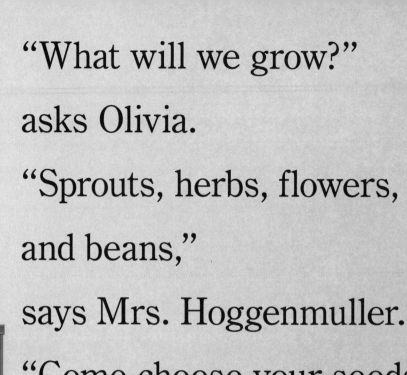

"What kind of seeds
are these?" asks Olivia.
"I do not know,"
says Mrs. Hoggenmuller.

"These are surprise seeds."

At home Olivia digs in
her yard.
Perry helps her dig.

"This is going to be the best surprise garden ever," she tells Julian.

"Did you know that talking to plants can help them grow faster?" asks Father.

"I can do that!" says Olivia.

"Hello, plants," says Olivia.
"I hope that you grow
so I will know what you are."

Olivia tells her plants
lots of stories.
She shows her plants
how she rides a scooter.
She sings songs to her
plants.

Oh no!
Perry is digging a hole
right where Olivia planted
her seeds.

"Oh, Perry!" says Olivia.
"I will just have to
plant more seeds.
And I will have to be even
more patient."

"Look!" says Olivia.
She holds up a bone.
"I think it is a
dinosaur bone."

"I am not sure," says Julian.

"I found a dinosaur bone
in my garden,"
says Olivia at school.
"I do not think that is

a dinosaur bone,"
says Mrs. Hoggenmuller.
"I think it is a dog toy.
Look! It is attracting flies."

Back at her house,
Olivia checks on her plants.
"My surprise seeds have
grown into surprise plants!"

All of the children bring
their plants to school.
"This is my surprise plant!"
says Olivia.

Snap!

Olivia's plant closes around
a fly.

"That is a Venus flytrap,"
says Mrs. Hoggenmuller.
"I will call it a surprise plant,"
says Olivia.
"That fly sure looked
surprised!"

"You did a wonderful job with your garden," says Father at bedtime. "I do not think we will have any more flies," says Olivia. "Good night, Olivia!"

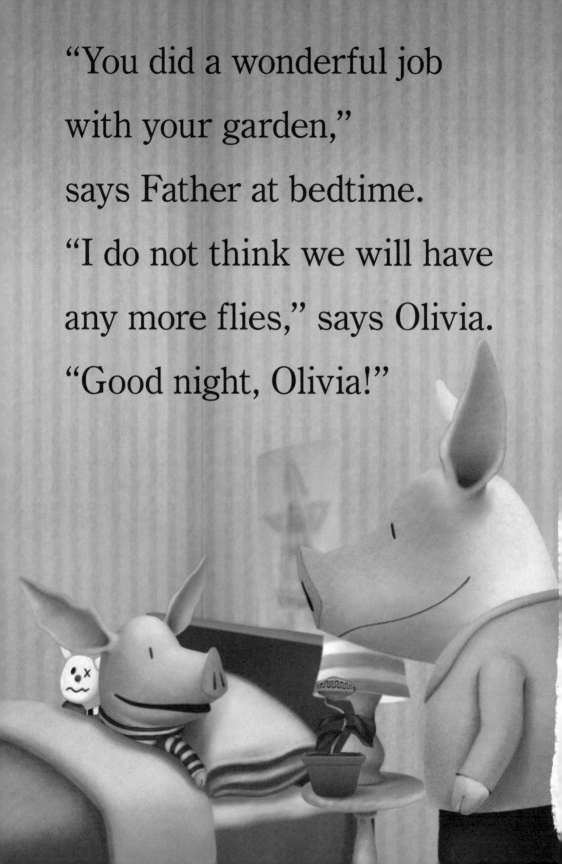